# No Time Like Snow Time!

## Written and illustrated by
### sixth graders at St. Mary's Public School in Trenton, Illinois

**Teacher: Amy Woods**

Lindsey Arnold, Trina Black, Amber Boulanger, Stefanie Brown, Alicia Crow, Brandon Deiters, Christina Green, Cindy Gullo, Alicia Hoerner, Kollin Huelsmann, Nikki Kohlbrecher, Shalan Lake, Nick Lercher, Bryan Litteken, Jessica McCann, Brandon Oglesby, Adrian Ramirez, Matt Reilman, Richard Rohe, Troy Schrage, Jennifer Spihlman, Kahla Thornton, Amanda Timmermann, Sheri Timmermann, Jason Totten, Shane Walden, Lynn Zimmers

One winter day at school, we were outside at recess time building a snowman from the first snowfall that year. We were having so much fun that we wished even more snow would fall!

(Little did we know that our wish would more than come true.)

Later that morning, while Mrs. Van Gogh was teaching us to paint in art class, it began to snow.  And snow.  And snow. Snow, snow, snow!

We looked out the window.  The snow was so high that it measured fifteen-kids tall!

Since the buses couldn't get through to take us home, it was obvious that we were snowed in at school for the night.

Teachers fainted, the principal cried, and the kids cheered!

**W**e all had to find something to do with our time. The first and second graders watched movies while they munched on popcorn.

**W**e, the third graders, went to the school library.  After we read books, we stacked them around our teacher, who had fainted earlier.

The fifth and sixth graders were using salt shakers to try to melt the snow.

The kindergartners, not knowing that salt melted the snow, used pepper instead.  It just turned the snow gray and black.

**A**t dinnertime, the principal rode by on his snowmobile. He handed off three pizzas to each classroom through the top window. Since the school cooks had left earlier in the day, this was a welcome treat!

For dessert, the fourth graders went to each classroom making snow cones. They used cups to dig snow out of the windows and flavorings from the cafeteria. Each kid in the school ate three snow cones!

After we ate, we were full and tired. The teachers walked up and down the rows saying, "Bedtime!"

We all lay down to sleep. Many of us were telling each other, "Night, night," or "See you in the morning."

When we woke up the next morning and tried to open the front doors, they magically opened!  The sidewalks were cleared.  Finally, we were able to go home.

"Hooray!" we shouted, as we ran back inside to grab our coats.

**A**s we were leaving, we noticed that the snowman we had built earlier had a shovel in his hand and a mysterious smile on his face!

# Kids Are Authors™ Competition
*Books written by children for children*

The Kids Are Authors™ Competition was established in 1986 to encourage children to read and to become involved in the creative process of writing. Since then, thousands of children have written and illustrated picture books as participants in the Kids Are Authors™ Competition. The winning books in the annual competition are published by Willowisp Press® and are distributed by PAGES Book Fairs throughout the United States.

For the **official rules** on the Kids Are Authors™ Competition or information on **how to order** Kids Are Authors™ books, write to:

## Kids Are Authors™ Competition

801 94th Avenue North

St. Petersburg, Florida 33702